W9-AWQ-120

SHADOWS

April Pulley Sayre

illustrated by

Harvey Stevenson

Henry Holt and Company · New York

Henry Holt and Company, LLC, *Publishers since 1866*
115 West 18th Street, New York, New York 10011

Henry Holt is a registered trademark of Henry Holt and Company, LLC
Text copyright © 2002 by April Pulley Sayre
Illustrations copyright © 2002 by Harvey Stevenson
All rights reserved.
Distributed in Canada by H. B. Fenn and Company Ltd.

Library of Congress Cataloging-in-Publication Data
Sayre, April Pulley. Shadows / April Pulley Sayre;
illustrated by Harvey Stevenson
Summary: Rhyming text describes the search of two young friends
for shadows in the everyday world.
[1. Shadows—Fiction. 2. Stories in rhyme.] I. Stevenson, Harvey, ill.
II. Title. PZ8.3.S2737 Sh 2002 [E]—dc21 2001000196

ISBN 0-8050-6059-6 / First Edition—2002 / Designed by Donna Mark
Printed in the United States of America on acid-free paper. ∞
10 9 8 7 6 5 4 3 2 1

The artist used acrylics on 300-gram Vinci paper to create
the illustrations for this book.

In honor of
Christine Dixon Vallevona,
who shared her joy and
love of nature   —A. P. S.

For Rebecca Schaffer,
with love   —H. S.

Searching for shadows,
we run,
hop!
STARE . . .

at lots of shadows
here
and
there.

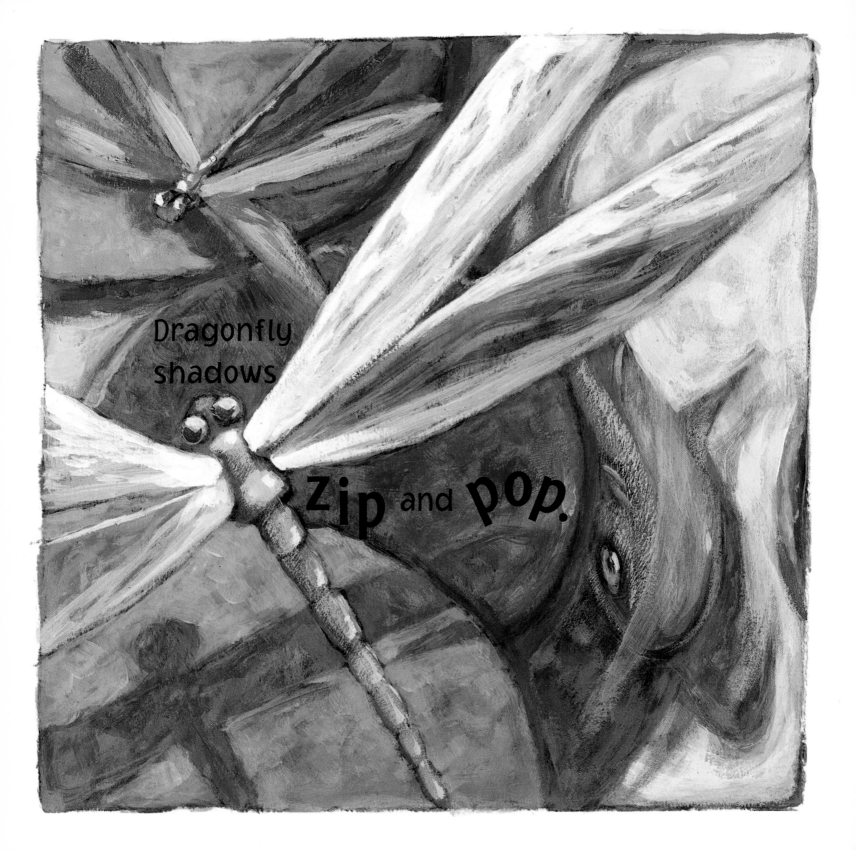

Dragonfly
shadows

Zip and pop.

Running horse shadows never STOP.

Our shadowy shapes
shift as we dance.
Leg kick! Leg kick!

Prance, prance, prance!

My friend catches my shadow's hand.

Hand in shadow
we **walk**
the sand.

A ball and its shadow

fa**ll**

and

meet,

rolling to my shadow's feet.

But later they've moved on the hot sidewalk.

A man keeps a shadow
under his hat.

An umbrella opens.
A shadow falls.

Splat!

Clouds move in—
sponging shadows a w a y.

But the shadows return with the sun. **Let's play!**

Hand shadows hop
through the **tall** green grass.

Underwater shadows
follow four *FAST* bass.

Toe shadows walk
the **gravelly** creek.

Sudden scary shadows
make us **SHRIEK!**

Bird shadows **skim**
over shrubs and rocks.

Sundial shadows **turn** like clocks.

Tree shadows
make **cool** spots to rest.

Sundial shadows **turn** like clocks.

Tree shadows
make **cool** spots to rest.

I think I like
these **shadows** best.